Snuggle

A M/F Demon Teddy Bear Romance

Yarn & Monsters
Book 2

Sabrina Cross

*To everyone who has spent the last month saying
"I Told
You So."
Fuck You.
Also, I love you.*

Author's Note

This is a sentient object romance. Humans will be getting it on with sentient objects. Don't worry, everyone is gleefully consenting.

If you read the last three sentences and think that's not for you, that's okay. There is still time to put this book down and walk away. No one will blame you. It's the sane thing to do.

But if you're going to stick around please be aware of the following:

Graphic sexual activity (oral, vaginal, anal), sex with an inanimate object, use of sex toys, abusive relationship recovery, mild child abuse (yelling), physical altercation of parents in front of children (grabbing), death threats of a parent in front of children (by a non-parent).

If you feel I am missing anything please reach out to me at authorsabrinacross@gmail.com and let me know. A complete list can be found at www.sabrinacross.com

Chapter One

It is a truth universally acknowledged that men suck.

Like really suck.

But not in a good 'suck my clit until I come' way but the terrible 'are completely useless for anything, way.

Case in point? My ex-husband Tyler.

The man waits until two days before Thanksgiving thou starts to tell me he's taking the kids for *his* visitation time. They're going to fly down to visit his parents in Florida and he and his girlfriend are going to take the girls to Disney World.

Never mind that he's missed his last six weekends, has never taken them mid-week, and has never cared about any holidays in the past. But no, his new girlfriend was keen to meet his parents and girls and they thought a family trip would be so much fun.

Thoughts and prayers, bitches.

Traveling by car with two kids under ten is a

nightmare hellscape. I didn't even want to imagine what flying with them would be like. I wasn't that desperate to go anywhere or see anyone.

Tyler had decided to ignore my warnings about traveling with kids. He wrote off my concerns about the girls meeting his new girlfriend so soon, especially with the ink on our divorce decree barely dry. He just told me to have them ready to be picked up on Tuesday after school and hung up.

Asshole.

What I'd ever seen in him was a mystery. He'd made the last seven years of my life misery.

I supposed it was good practice for when I ended up in Hell.

And that was literal Hell. Not some metaphorical place or somewhere people thought of as Hell, like the DMV. I meant the actual fire and brimstone place.

A friend of mine talked a group of us into doing a spell to find true love a couple of months back. It wasn't my cup of tea, but Violet can be very persuasive when she wants to and I wanted to support my unhappily single friend.

Stupid, stupid me. Instead, what I'd done was accidentally signed a deal with the devil that meant I had a year to find true love or I'd end up in Hell at the end of the year. I have two kids to raise and a shitty ex-husband. I didn't have time to go to Hell.

The worst part was the fact we were supposedly each being assigned a demon to "assist" us in finding true love. I figured there was some trap there that I was missing, but since my demon never showed up, I wasn't sure what it could be.

Especially since my best friend, Clover, went and fell in love with her demon. She was absolutely worthless when it came to trying to get information about the deal with the devil and the demons in general. All she'd say was that they needed a vessel. The vessel, or poppet, was made by Clover using magical crochet hooks. Something she'd learned when she'd mistakenly used the magical hooks to make the most ridiculous candy corn hooker on the planet and ended up sticking her demon inside of it.

No, she wasn't in love with the candy corn. Candy, was able to regain her true form after they'd fallen in love.

Since I had little interest in a demon babysitter, I'd given Clover the challenge of making me a life-sized teddy bear. I figured it'd take her forever to crochet me something that large.

What I didn't take into consideration was how fast Clover was at crochet, and how much more time she had on her hands now that Candy had taken over the business side of the business Clover ran.

Now I had a five-foot-tall stuffed bear sitting in the spare chair in my office. The girls thought he was cute and constantly wanted to play with him. The very sight of him filled me with dread.

According to Clover and Candy, we would

each meet our true love — what a gag phrase — sometime before the year was up and it was up to us to realize who they were and to get them to fall in love with us. Super easy. Absolutely not the most outrageous deal ever made.

Once I was sure I wasn't going to be dragged kicking and screaming to Hell, I was going to strangle Violet. The only thing keeping her alive was that she was still researching loopholes to our deal, trying to find non-love related ways out of it.

If I did end up in Hell, I was going to kick Lucifer's ass until he sent me back to Earth and my kids just to be rid of me. No way was I leaving their raising to Tyler and his dimwit assistant/girlfriend.

It had taken everything in me to let the kids into the car. Tyler was going to be terrible. He had no patience for the girls and their quirks and big personalities. Jessica hadn't seemed like she was capable of handling a poodle, let alone two excited kids.

But Tyler had the big lawyer job with the big lawyer pay and the big expensive divorce attorney who would make my life miserable just on principle if I didn't let him fulfill his little "perfect family" weekend.

I watched the car disappear down the driveway and slumped against the door frame.

"Good grief, I thought they would never leave." The deep voice came from behind me, causing me to jump.

I spun around and there, on the stairs, stood

the five-foot-tall stuffed bear. It was a light brown color with large black button eyes, its nose and mouth had been embroidered on.

If I didn't know better, I would have assumed someone had climbed inside of the bear and was trying to scare me. But I did know better.

I sighed and closed the door before leaning against it. My hands were flat against the door behind my back. I needed to keep myself from picking up the first thing I could and start pelting that damn teddy bear.

"I take it you're my demon."

Chapter Two

"I guess that makes you my human."

The voice that came out of the teddy bear was unnaturally deep. It made the hair on my body stand on end and I fought the urge to rub my hands up and down my arms to settle it. I didn't want to show any weakness. I wouldn't let the thing know it was getting to me.

"Well, I wouldn't."

The bear tilted its head in question.

"I'm not your anything."

"Mmmm, so tough." I could feel his black eyes boring into me. "It would be more convincing if I couldn't smell your fear from here."

I straightened away from the door, my back straight as I stared it down. Okay, yeah, I was terrified. There was a five-foot teddy bear roughly the same width as me and possessed by a demon standing on my stairs. Of course, I was scared. Any sane person would be.

But he didn't need to point it out. Sheesh.

"Try not breathing. It would keep you from smelling me." Oh goddess, why was I baiting the demon? I had children to raise, I couldn't get myself killed.

Instead of striking out at me, the demon threw back his fluffy teddy head and laughed. The boom of it was enough to reverberate in my chest. Like the loud thump of a bass in a bar on a Friday night. Something I'd been experiencing far too often since this damn deal with the devil happened.

"Oh, you are a fierce little thing. I think I'm going to enjoy you."

"I am five inches taller than you." I pointed out.

"In this form, maybe." He looked down at himself and poked his rounded belly with his rounded arm. "Why did you choose this form?

I shrugged, "Hard to be intimidated by a child's plaything."

"Oh yes, I'm going to enjoy you." This time, it sounded less amused and more like a threat.

That was fine. I had a narcissistic ex-husband and had worked in customer service for a decade. I could handle some vague threats.

"Well, this has been fun. But I have to get to work or else I won't be able to eat and weirdly, little girls enjoy things like food. You...do whatever the heck you want, I guess. Not like I could stop you."

I tried to walk up the stairs and edge around him, he but put an arm out to block my path.

When I tried to step back down, he blocked me in. Using his other arm and his round belly, he pinned me to the handrail.

"Shouldn't you be focused on your deal with Lucifer? Time is running out." Heat emanated off his soft, chenille body.

It was like standing a little too close to a fire. I could tell he was trying to be intimidating, and maybe I should have been somewhat intimidated. I mean, hello, demon. But the teddy bear was five inches shorter than me and just so damn adorable I couldn't take it seriously. Instead, I did the only thing I could do in that situation.

I laughed.

I laughed until my body shook. I laughed until the bear took a step back to stare up at me and I knew it was thinking I was crazy, which just made me laugh harder. I was being judged by a giant teddy bear. Of course, I was going to laugh. I laughed until tears streamed down my face.

Then I wasn't laughing anymore. I was sobbing. I was sliding down the banister to sit on the stair and put my head between my knees as I cried. It was all so ridiculous and stupid, and I was sick and tired of it all.

Heat flared at my side a moment before an arm wrapped around my back, rubbing up and down. Oh, okay. Because things couldn't get more ridiculous, now the demon was soothing me? Sure. Why not?

"I take it all back." The demon told me. "You're absolutely insane."

Wiping my eyes against my shirt sleeve, I sat up and nodded. "Yeah, probably. I mean, if anyone saw me talking to a life-sized teddy bear, they'd probably put me in the loony bin. Especially if I told them I wasn't talking to myself, but a bear possessed by a demon. When one's life is this insane, you either embrace the insanity, or you sink under the weight of it. I refuse to sink."

"Is that so, little warrior?" The growl was back in his voice, but it wasn't scary this time. I actually found it oddly comforting. Oh gods, I was finding a demon comforting. Someone should probably call the guys with the butterfly nets to put me out of my misery, after all.

Chapter Three

"What do I call you?" I asked the demon when I came downstairs later. After our awkward interlude on the stairs, I'd dashed up to my office and locked myself in for the morning. The demon had allowed it. I had no delusions about his ability to stop me if he had wanted to.

I had found him in the kitchen staring at the coffee machine with what I guessed was his angry face. It was hard to tell with the black button eyes.

"My name is Phinarax. I am a soldier in one of Asmodeus' many legions."

"Cool, cool. I'm just gonna call you Phin."

"My name is Phinarax." The deep growl was back in his voice. The sound reverberated through me. I pressed a hand to my stomach but didn't back down.

We stood glaring at each other across the center island. His name was a stupid thing to pick an argument about, but I really needed a win right that moment. I'd spent all morning on the phone with one angry customer after another. Usually, my job was to post payments made. But I'd been loaned out to another department doing collections, and I hated every moment. I was not a confrontational person by nature, and the constant barrage had drained me.

"Let me call you Phin and I'll make a pot of coffee." I was going to make the pot of coffee anyway, but he didn't need to know that.

He nodded and stepped aside. We switched positions, placing me next to the coffeepot. Phin watched carefully as I filled the pot and poured the water into the reservoir and dumped the coffee into the filter. I suddenly remembered; Candy drank coffee too. Maybe it was a demon thing.

"We must talk about your plans. I have better things to do than sit here babysitting a mortal and the sooner you find your mate, the better off everyone will be."

"What if I don't want a mate? What if I have decided I have zero interest in finding a new man and want to die an old lady and eventually get eaten by my many, many cats?" The idea had some appeal to it. Okay, probably not the eaten by cats thing, but I couldn't blame animals for doing what came naturally.

Phin harrumphed, clearly unimpressed with my plan.

I ignored him in favor of getting two mugs down from the cabinet. Pausing the machine, I poured out two cups before returning the carafe and turning it back on. I dumped an unhealthy amount of powdered chocolate creamer into my cup and stirred it.

As soon as I turned around, I could almost see the glare Phin was giving me. Instead of scaring me, as being glared at by a demon should have done, I found a bit of amusement in irritating him.

"You signed a deal. You will not live to old age if you do not find your mate. A body cannot live without its soul, and Lucifer will claim yours at the end of the year you were allotted."

"What does Lucifer even want with my soul? I'm boring, not good for much. I'm practically worthless." All things I had been told by my ex-husband. I didn't believe him, anymore, but if the demon thought I had no value, maybe he would let me be.

Phin snorted and picked up his mug between his two bear paws. I watched in fascinated horror as he dumped the coffee where his mouth was. All of it. The whole mug at once.

Instead of pouring down the front of him and pooling on the floor as I had expected it to have done, it had just disappeared. There was no evidence that coffee had ever been there. If I hadn't poured the mug myself, I would have thought he had faked it.

"How did you do that?"

"Do what?"

I gestured to his empty mug. "Drink the coffee."

"Demon. Magic. I may be stuck in this ridiculous body, but I am not without my abilities." He looked down at the empty mug. "And that swamp water was not coffee."

I chose to ignore the jab at my perfectly fine coffee and thought about the second part. I knew Candy had certain abilities, but I hadn't asked details and Clover hadn't shared a whole lot. Just that Candy was capable of being places where the stuffed candy corn shouldn't have been able to get and had seemed to read Clover's mind at times.

The mind reading bothered me more than anything. I'd spent years with someone else's voice in my head. I didn't want anyone else up there now that I'd finally stopped hearing Tyler every time I turned around.

Tyler had spent so much time telling me I was stupid, useless, pathetic. That I couldn't do anything right. That I would never be able to exist without him, I had started to believe it. I had started hearing his voice every time I wanted to try something new or thought about leaving.

It had taken six months of weekly therapy appointments to get his voice out of my brain, and I refused to let anyone else have that power over me again.

"As for your soul, every soul has power and serves a purpose. There is no such thing as a worthless soul. The only way out of this bargain is to fulfill the terms of it. Until then you're stuck with me and I'm stuck with you. So, hurry the fuck up and find your mate already."

"If you think it's so easy, you find him. I just divorced a narcissist. Clearly, I'm terrible at the whole thing." I set my now empty mug down in the sink and crossed my arms around my stomach.

"I'm a five-foot teddy bear. Just how to you expect me to do that?"

It wasn't a no.

"That's your problem. I have to get back to work." I walked out of the kitchen and left the demon there to try to figure out how to find me a soul mate.

Best of luck to him.

I was pretty sure my soul mate didn't exist.

Chapter Four

"I have found you a date." Phin said with a large amount of smugness when I came out of my office for the day. "You will meet him tonight. You will not go dressed like that."

I rolled my eyes and headed for the stairs and the kitchen. I was not interested in meeting whoever Phin had pulled out of his magical hat. I wasn't interested in anything that wasn't the left-over pizza in my fridge and a bottle of wine.

"Did you hear me?" Phin waddled into the room. His legs were just large enough to support his form, and it was actually quite amusing watching him walk.

"Yep. No. Not happening. Pizza, hot bath, and too much wine is happening. Probably a romance novel or some bad TV too, if I can find the energy for it." I took a bite of the cold, leftover pizza. "What I don't have the energy for is some rando hookup. Plus, I have serious doubts about the type of person you could dig up in less than a day."

Phin stared at me for the longest time while I ate my pizza. I used to be self-conscious about that sort of thing, but I had two kids and was happy when I got to eat a full meal without having to get up and get someone something.

Eventually he nodded and walked out of the room.

Okay then...

I finished my second slice of pizza, tossed the box in the trash, and refilled my wine glass before heading back upstairs. I was going to take a hot bath until my skin pruned and the water went cold. Then I was going to crawl into bed and watch something mindless until I fell asleep.

Except, I got up to the bathroom and found Phin in there. The room was steamy and smelled softly of lavender and vanilla. It wasn't my favorite of the bath salts I owned, but it was nice.

"What is this?" I asked, setting my glass of wine on the counter.

"You said you wanted a bath. You looked like you could use one. So, I made you a bath. You could try thank you."

"Thank you." I said automatically. It was more habit than any actual gratitude. I was still too confused for gratitude.

I stood there, taking in the steaming water, the trio of candles flickering on the back of the toilet, the fluffy towel on the toilet seat. My ereader was sitting on top of the towel, within reach of the tub.

It was perfect. Absolutely perfect.

"I'll let you get to it," Phin said. waddling past me and out the door. "Enjoy."

I closed the door behind him and stripped in a daze. What the hell was this? It didn't make any sense. Why had the demon put so much effort into this? Why had he bothered at all?

I climbed into the tub. The water was just this side of too warm, just the way I liked it. I leaned back against the tub and for the second time that day, I burst into tears.

After my bath, I did my best to avoid Phin. I headed straight to my bedroom to put on my soft cotton sleep shorts and a T-shirt. I combed out my hair and tied it back in a loose braid so it wouldn't tangle in my sleep.

I settled myself under my plush weighted blanket, propped against the headboard reading when the door opened and Phin walked in.

"Knocking exists."

"I knew you'd tell me no." He tipped over awkwardly to sit on the bed next to me. "I don't like no."

"Who does?" I shifted over to allow him more room. I could have made a bigger deal of it, but frankly I was tired. It had been a long and emotionally draining day and I just wasn't in the mood to fight anymore.

The bath and the cry had both done wonders to help release most of the tension of the day, but now I was just drained. I was an empty shell and was completely ready to check out.

"You can't avoid men forever," Phin said, his gaze on the blank TV screen.

"No, not forever. Just until I don't hate them on principle anymore. Is that too much to ask?" That was the crux of the matter, really. It had been six months since my divorce was final. Before that, it had been months of custody battles, arguments over assets, pettiness, and finally some light blackmail. The thought of dating was exhausting. And honestly, a little nauseating. I just wanted some time to be me.

"It doesn't matter," I said. "I don't have the time I need, do I?" I dropped my kindle on my bedside table and turned off the light.

I turned to my side and pulled the blanket up to my face. "You can watch TV or do whatever it is demons do at night. I'm going to sleep."

"I'm good here." Phin wiggled a little bit, settling deeper into the bed.

"You're not sleeping here!"

"I don't sleep."

I flipped over to glare at him. "Well, you're sure as hell not going to sit there and watch me sleep all night. Go do something."

He waved his arms around. His silly, bear arms without any fingers or thumbs. "Like what?

Sure, I have some powers, but I'm still limited by this form."

"I don't know!" I flailed my own arm at him. "Look. Not only is sitting there watching me sleep creepy as hell, I am tired and tense and just want a great orgasm and some sleep. And I'm sure as hell not masturbating while you're in here."

I covered my face with my hand. I couldn't believe I just told him that. But maybe it would work, and he would go away.

No such luck.

"I could help you with that."

"With what?" Not believing for one moment he was suggesting what I thought he was suggesting.

"Lust demon. I guarantee I can get you off better than anyone you've ever met, including yourself."

I laughed. I'd heard that before. I hadn't been a virgin before marrying Tyler. Every man boasted about his, usually lackluster, abilities to get me off and every one had been barely adequate.

"I could prove it to you. Without even touching you." He was staring down at me and there was an intensity in those button eyes that sent a shiver down my spine and warmed my skin. He used one paw to push some loose hair away from my face. "If you're not screaming out to your god within minutes I'll leave you alone."

"And if I am?" My voice was low and rough and I hardly recognized it.

"Well then, we both win. Don't we, little warrior?"

There wasn't much of an argument to be made. Or if there was, I wasn't capable of making it. It'd been a year since someone else had touched me, longer since someone else had made me come. This demon said he could do it without laying a paw on me and I wanted to see if he was actually capable.

Okay, and I really wanted that orgasm.

"Prove it."

Chapter Five

I didn't know what I expected, but it certainly wasn't the sudden flood of heat to my clit. It wasn't the feel of something spreading my lower lips and penetrating me. My vagina stretched around the invisible intrusion. I rolled onto my back, my legs widened without a thought.

I stared at Phin, wanting more of whatever he was doing to me. It was good, but it wasn't nearly enough. The invisible cock moved deeper, filling every last part of me, and I moaned, the sound unbidden. I clasped a hand over my mouth, but it was immediately pulled away by some invisible force. Both wrists pinned to the bed at my sides.

"Nuh-uh-uh, I can't win our bargain if you're hiding those sweet little sounds," Phin said, his eyes on my face. His normally low growl of a voice was practically gravel. I could feel the sound of it throughout my whole body. My clit throbbed in time to the beat of it, and I tilted my hips into the sensation.

I had barely recovered from that feeling when heat so intense flooded my clit at the same time the invisible cock moved inside me.

I moaned at the slow, steady thrusts. It was maddening. The phallus retreated nearly entirely before moving achingly slow all of the way in to press against my cervix, adding a nearly painful edge to the pleasure.

It wasn't enough.

"You can take more now, right, little warrior?" I moaned, nodding rapidly. Needing whatever 'more' entailed. I hoped it meant speeding up. I hoped it might involve my aching nipples.

It didn't.

There was a slow, steady stretch to my back entrance.

"What!" I yelped, arching. Except, I was no longer sure if I was trying to move away from the foreign sensation or to it.

"Don't you like it?" Both invisible phalluses started moving. The one in my rear pushing deeper while the one in my cunt pulled out. They began a slow thrust, moving so that one hole was always empty while the other was filled.

"Isn't it such a wonderful feeling? Being so very stretched and full?"

I nodded quickly, reveling in sensation. "Yes!" My voice was a high gasp.

"Look at you using your words," Phin said. "Such a good girl."

The cocks started moving faster, and I arched into the air, my body bowing up. The feeling was overwhelming, but somehow not enough. As they increased in speed, moans started streaming out of my mouth. A steady sound, rising in volume.

"Oh my," I bit my lip, keeping gods' name out of my mouth. I wouldn't let him win that easily.

"Oh, your what, little warrior?"

"Nothing." I moaned. I was thrusting into the air, constantly chasing that feeling of being full. "Oh my, nothing."

"Poor girl, you seem to be having an issue. Do you need more?"

I nodded vigorously, but nothing changed. It was still the steady thrust of one pressing in and one retreating.

"Use your words, warrior."

"Yes, goddess yes! I need more." I was prepared to beg if it would get me what I needed. Pleasure was pooled low in my stomach, my muscles tight. My skin was damp with a sheen of sweat and I was on fire. Every part of me was riding the edge.

"Oh yes, such a good, good girl." The words shivered through me. I'd never thought of needing praise in bed, but something about the words ratcheted my pleasure higher.

Before I could think too hard about it, both of the invisible phalluses pulled nearly out of me before slamming in at the same time. I was full. So, so full. My full body arched away from the bed. The only thing keeping me in place were the invisible restraints around my wrists. I was writhing as heat flooded my entire body.

"Oh my god, oh my god, oh my god," I chanted, not caring a whit that Phin had won our bet. His smugness would be worth this. My entire body strung tight, my eyes shut, my hips moving; trying to get just the smallest amount of friction on my clit. I was so close.

Suddenly, a wave of heat flooded my clit. Lights exploded behind my eyes; my pussy clenched around whatever that invisible phallus was. I was coming so hard it almost hurt. My body collapsed to the bed and I could feel my come leaking down between my legs. The pressure in my vagina and anus disappeared, and my arms were freed. The blanket moved itself up from the end of the bed and over me. I hadn't even realized I had knocked it off.

"You win." I whispered, my mouth dry. My eyelids were too heavy to lift and the weight of the blanket was a gentle pressure lulling me to sleep.

"No, little warrior." Phin's paw swept my hair back from my face. "I'm pretty sure we both won that round."

Chapter Six

I woke up wrapped around Phin. At some point in the night, I had lost my blanket and thrown my arm and leg over him. I would have thought I would have gotten cold, the whole November in Michigan thing, but he generated so much heat it was like hugging a furnace.

I jerked back and away from him, embarrassed and uncomfortable with the situation. Snuggling any stranger would have been awkward. Snuggling a minion of Lucifer here to help shepherd my soul to Hell? Even my subconscious should have known better than that!

"Good morning. Is today the day you're finally going to take finding a mate seriously?" Phin asked, rising to sit awkwardly on the bed. I had a moment of sympathy for him, being stuck in such a large and awkward body. Even standing was defying gravity. I wondered what he looked like without the bear suit.

Candy had never shared her demon form,

though Clover said she was more gorgeous as a demon than a human. I found that hard to believe because Candy was a straight ten in her human form.

Would Phin be the same way?

Lust demons had to be attractive to draw in their prey, right? It would make sense he was gorgeous. But what about his demon form? All I knew about demons came from movies and books, and few of them were attractive.

And why the hell was I even thinking about how he normally looked? One good orgasm and suddenly I'm willing to forget that he's here to take me to Hell and away from my kids? No.

"No. Today is the day I'm going to take a shower and go to work. I told you. I don't have time for men."

"You need to make time." He sounded tired of me already. Maybe Tyler had been right about my ability to annoy people.

"I know you think I'm a trap, but I swear I have no other purpose than to keep you safe and help you find your mate. That's it."

"Why?" That was the real question, right?

Why were demons so invested in our future happiness? Why were they helping to keep us out of Hell? Why did any of them care?

As far as I knew, Clover and I were the only two to get our demons so far, but Candy had said the same thing. That she was there to protect Clover and nothing else. But it didn't make any sense based on everything I had ever heard.

"It's not my place to question my lord. I just do as directed. He seems to have a special interest in your coven's future, but I don't know what it is."

Aweeeeeesome.

We'd captured the attention of the devil. That was cool. Not at all concerning. Seriously, just FML.

"I find it weird that two of you got your demons at the same time." Violet said, her voice coming through the phone I had propped up in front of me. We were on a group video chat during my lunch break. I was being cowardly and refusing to go downstairs and face Phin.

"You're just jealous you haven't seen your demon yet," Clover said. Candy leaned over to whisper something to her, and Clover grinned. I wanted in on the joke.

As suspicious as I was about the pairing, I couldn't deny that Clover was much happier. Or that Candy did seem to genuinely care for her happiness and well-being. Clover practically glowed these days.

"I don't find it interesting." Fern said. Her eyebrows were drawn together. "I don't find anything about this whole thing interesting. It's all terrible!"

"Not a fan of your demon?" Clover asked,

grinning at Candy. I kind of wanted to punch her in the face.

Fern's face pinched even more. I made a note to call her one-on-one after we got off the phone. She was clearly upset and these bozos (whom I loved dearly and would do anything for) were clearly not helping.

"I'm not a fan of having a demon babysitter. And I keep thinking about Grams coming by and somehow finding out. And then I'd have the priest and half the congregation in my house trying to perform an exorcism and we all know how those stories go." She was breathing heavily, her chest heaving in near hyperventilation speeds.

Of all of us, Fern was the only one with religious ties. Clover was a pagan. Violet was a lifelong agnostic. I was a recovering Baptist who hadn't been to church outside of the occasional family wedding since I was ten. Fern wasn't a 'Church every Sunday' kind of girl, but she definitely believed in God. It would make sense that having a demon as a houseguest would be the hardest on her.

Clover was trying to talk Fern down when there was a soft womp on my office door. I swung around in my chair just as it opened. I was prepared to yell at Phin but when I saw him, no words would come out. He stood in the doorway, balancing a baking sheet on his outstretched arms. There was a coffee mug, a glass of water, and a couple of bowls on the sheet.

"Hey guys, I've gotta go." I hung up before anyone could say anything. I looked back at Phin. "What's all of this?"

"You didn't come down for lunch." I got up and took the tray from him. I checked out the bowls. One contained beef stew that I knew had to have come from a can. The other had carrots and cut celery lining the outside with a healthy dollop of ranch dressing in the bottom. "You need to eat something."

I stared down at the tray. It hadn't taken much effort. Just warming up a can of stew and taking the pre-cut and washed veggies from the baggie I stored them in. I honestly couldn't think of the last time someone had done something so thoughtful for me.

Oh fuck. I was about to cry again. What was it about this demon that made me so emotional?

"Thank you." I moved back to my desk and set the tray down. "What have you been up to today?"

I hadn't really considered what he would do in my house all day while I worked. I really hadn't considered him much at all. Embarrassment over last night had kicked in and I'd been avoiding him. A little pathetic? Yes. But there it was.

"I found you a date for tonight. You can't skip this one. I also did some online shopping. And cleaned the kitchen before making you lunch."

"Okay, first, you don't dictate if I go on dates

or not. That isn't up to you. Second, why the hell did you clean my kitchen?"

Phin shrugged; the movement awkward in his body. "It needed doing. Are you done working yet?"

"No, just a lunch break." I glanced to the clock, "Which is almost over."

"I'll leave you to it then." He ambled out of the room, the door closing gently behind him without anyone touching it.

Oooookay, then.

I looked back at the baking sheet with my lunch on it. I couldn't stop the warm fuzzy feeling of someone taking care of me for a change. I picked up the fork and dug into the stew. It wasn't as good as homemade, but it was the best lunch I'd had in a long time.

Chapter Seven

P hin was waiting for me in the hall when I'd finished work for the day. I wasn't surprised. I'd known the talk about my date wasn't over. Phin had made it clear he wanted me to find my mate so he could get back to his life.

I wondered what it was demons did all day when they weren't stuck babysitting humans. Were the church stories true, where they spent all of eternity tormenting humans? It seemed like that would get boring after a while.

"No time for a bath tonight," Phin said. "I've laid out your clothes for you."

"I'm not a child. I don't need you to dress me."

"I hadn't offered to dress you. Though I assure you, in my normal form, you'd enjoy the experience. Sadly, I'm limited in this." He gestured at himself and I felt a flash of heat and a pang of sympathy.

I once again wondered what he really looked

like. After the previous night, I didn't doubt the boast he could make dressing me enjoyable.

"Assuming I was willing to go out tonight, which I'm really not, I can pick out my own damn clothes." Tyler had often picked out my clothes when we had to attend business functions. He always claimed that he needed his wife to look the part of a partner's wife. We both had to dress to the job he wanted. It hadn't escaped my notice that his new girlfriend dressed like the trophy she was, not the sedate classy he preferred me in.

Fucking men.

"Then pick out your own damn clothes! But you are going out. Violet and Fern will be here in about an hour." He stormed off toward the stairs. Well, as much as a giant teddy bear could storm.

I had to give the demon credit. He'd dragged my friends into it and now I couldn't bail. It was smart. Underhanded and manipulative, but smart.

I took a shower and wrapped myself in my fluffy robe before heading to my bedroom to see what a demon thought I should wear on my, apparently, group date. It could be nothing good.

I was surprised when I saw what Phin had laid out. It was a calf-length corduroy skirt in deep forest green. He'd paired it with a black long sleeve blouse that had a slight V-neck. A pair of black, low-heel ankle boots sat on the floor beside the bed. It wasn't an outfit I would have chosen for myself, but I couldn't fault his taste.

After getting dressed, I pulled my hair back

into a loose curving braid that hung down over one shoulder. I added a pair of silver hoop earrings and switched my wallet from my mom bag, to the small black crossbody I never used. It didn't have room for extra tablets or snacks, so it was pretty much useless in my daily life.

I had just finished my makeup when the doorbell rang. A weird part of me expected Phin to answer the door. But, of course, he wouldn't. He was a sentient teddy bear. His answering the door was insane, even if the people on the other side of it were expecting it.

Jogging down the stairs as fast as I dared in the skirt and heels, I shouted a goodbye to Phin. I grabbed my keys off of the hook by the door and met my friends on the porch.

"Damn girl, you're looking fine tonight." Violet said. She was short and curvy, wearing a pair of black pants and a dark orange sweater with a deep V-neck that made her boobs look great. Her hair was currently bright blue and pinned up in a messy updo that suited her. Fern was average height, about two inches taller than my five-five. She was cute with her blond curls hanging over her shoulders, wearing a dark red wrap sweater dress with long sleeves and fell just below her knees. She'd paired it with tall black boots.

"Look who's talking!" I said, directing them away from my door. "Where are we going tonight? Group date?"

"Worse." Fern said sullenly.

"Speed dating." Violet said with a shudder.

I stopped on the top step and gaped at them. "Why?!"

"According to the text we got from Phin," Fern started.

"Who knew demons could text?" Violet interrupted.

"Why wouldn't they be able to?" Fern asked, playing with the ends of her hair.

"Are there cell phones in Hell?" That was Violet.

"It's Hell. They probably invented cell phones." I started down the stairs toward the car. "Who else would invent something to tie all of humanity together in an epic doomscroll?"

There was silence as we all contemplated that as we got into the car. I waited until everyone was buckled and Violet was pulling out of my drive before returning to the question of why the heck we were going speed dating.

"According to Phin," Fern said, glaring at Violet. "You're being difficult about going out and setting you up with multiple guys at once increases the odds of you finding someone so he can go back home where it's never this cold and there aren't 'infernal women' to drive him crazy."

"The demon generates heat. What would he care about the cold?" I grumbled, sitting back, crossing my arms over my chest.

"And how would you know how much heat he generates?" Violet asked.

I loved my friends. They were amazing. They'd helped get me out of my marriage and through an unnecessarily complicated divorce. They loved my kids and were the aunts they didn't genetically have. I would do anything for them.

There was no fucking way I was telling them about the orgasm Phin gave me. Or waking up snuggled up on him this morning.

"Have you stood next to a demon? They're their own furnaces." I looked to Fern for confirmation.

"She has a point." Fern said. "Jax is very warm."

We didn't talk much during the short ride into town. Violet pulled up behind a brewery and found a parking spot in the surprisingly full lot. It was the night before Thanksgiving. Didn't people have better things to do?

Then again, I was a mother of two girls, a full-time worker, cursed by the devil, and I was still here.

"If this is half as bad as I think it's going to be," Violet said as we were walking to the door. "I'm cursing you. Pretty sure you can't curse a demon and he's your demon so it's your fault."

"Your logic is terrifying," I said.

"Plus, it was your spell that put us here. So really, if it's anyone's fault, it's yours." Fern coming in with the assist and the excellent use of logic.

"What she said." I stepped forward and pulled the door open. "Let the fun begin."

Chapter Eight

"Phinarax whatever your last name is," I hollered, storming through the door. "You are the worst demon on this planet and I'm going to kick your ass back to Hell!"

I threw my purse and keys on the hallway table and stormed into the kitchen, determined to find the demon and wring his neck. I had never been more humiliated in my life, and I'd been married to Tyler for seven years!

Phin was in my room, propped against the headboard and watching something on the TV. I stormed up to him and punched him in his soft, squishy belly.

"What the bloody hell was that for?" He yelled, sitting upright.

"You sent us to a *gay and lesbian* speed dating event!" I screamed, punching him again. "We stroll in all casual as can be and find out all of the well-dressed, attractive men were *gay!*"

Look, we had nothing against gays or lesbians.

Clover was bisexual and cohabitating with a female demon. We didn't judge. But none of the three of us was anything but straight.

We'd seen the banner about thirty seconds after we'd walked in and realized what the event actually was. Unfortunately, the event host had already spotted us and was rushing over to greet us. We'd ended up playing dumb, saying we didn't realize there was a private event. We were not very convincing. I was sure the host knew we'd showed up at the wrong event.

I went to hit Phin again, but he caught my hand between his arms in a shockingly firm grip. He used my surprise and momentum to pull me down on top of him. Before I'd registered that position, he'd flipped us so I was under him. He was surprisingly solid for something made out of yarn and fluff. Impossibly heavy and firm against me.

"Oh, little warrior," Phin said, pinning my arm to the bed with one paw. "I let you have two. You shouldn't have been greedy and gone for a third hit. I'm benevolent, but I'm no masochist." He nuzzled his face into my neck.

For one wild moment, I wished he could bite me. Sink his teeth into my neck over and over again. Nibble his way up to my ear or down to my collarbone. But that was insane. He was a demon! He was a comically unbalanced crochet teddy bear! There was no reason I should be enjoying the situation.

"Will you get off of me?" I began to struggle,

wondering at the fact I couldn't budge the shorter, lighter stuffed animal a centimeter.

"I think I'm going to return the favor and give you three." He was completely unphased by my struggle. Using magic against me was totally unfair.

"You'd hit a girl?" I was going for snarky but it came out more girly. Was I *flirting* with the demon?

"No, little warrior. I'm not going to hit you." He pressed his hips down to me. There was no bulge where a man's penis would be but the pressure was still a jolt to my center. "I'm going to make you give me three orgasms."

He lacked hips but he rotated his base against me. At some point he'd worked his way between my legs and his body was pressing against my center. My skirt was stretched between us, dulling the sensation. I wriggled down a little to try to move it. I realized what I was doing and stopped myself.

"I'm going to pin you to the bed and push you over the edge. I'm going to do it over, and over again." The growl was back in his voice and shivering through my body. I caught a moan in my throat, desperately trying to swallow back the sound.

"Now you're going to stay right here." The invisible straps were back around my wrists, pinning them together and over my head. "And I'm going to work you over until you can't remember anything but my name."

He pulled away, and I whined, missing the sensation I had been getting, muted as they were. I gasped when Phin used his paws to shove my skirt up over my hips until my black lace underwear were exposed. He stared down at me for a moment before bringing his paw against my pussy and pressing firmly into my clit. He stopped there, completely still.

After a moment, I couldn't take it anymore and moved my hips against him. I wiggled against his paw, taking the sensations I needed from him. He chuckled, the sound dark and low. It zipped through me, making me shudder lightly against his paw.

"That's it, warrior. Take what you need." He pressed harder against me, making me moan. He leaned forward and nuzzled his nose against my boob. His firm movements scraped the lace of my bra against my peaked nipple. I moved my hips faster against him, nearing the edge and desperately wanting to go over it.

Phin started moving his arm firmly against me. The added pressure and movement were enough to send pleasure bursting over me. Lights flickered behind my eyes as my orgasm hit me. My body was bowed tight, but I couldn't help the whine as my pussy clenched on nothing.

"That's one." Phin said in my ear. His growl reverberated through my chest. "Just two more to go, little warrior."

Oh, goddess.

He kept moving his paw against my overly-sensitive clit. I struggled to move away, but he followed me. It was too much; it was not nearly enough. I whined, needing relief, needing more, just needing.

"What's wrong, warrior?" He pressed up on one arm to look down at me while keeping his other paw firmly against my cunt. "Use your words."

"Can't. Too much." I panted the words.

"You can and you will." He rubbed faster. "I think I know what you need. Ask nicely and I'll give it to you. I'll give you everything you need."

"Please," I begged. "Please, more. Not enough. Please!"

"That's my good girl." Suddenly my vagina was stretched around something firm and wide. My inner muscles clenched hard around it, swiftly sending me over the edge again.

I came down slowly, panting, as my body settled back into the bed. I knew I looked a mess. My hair had come loose from my braid, my shirt was bunched up under my breasts. My skirt was currently acting as a belt around my waist. I was sweaty and struggling to keep my eyes open. I had never been more spent in my life.

"Good job, little warrior. Just one more to go."

"I can't," I moaned. My throat was raw, and I desperately needed some water. "Can't. No more."

"It wouldn't be punishment if it was all fun and games, now would it, little warrior?" Phin pushed up so he was sitting back between my splayed legs. His were awkwardly laying on the bed behind him. "You will give me one more and you're going to scream my name when you do it."

The invisible phallus started moving. So, so slowly. It was so large I could feel it against every part of my vagina. It scraped against my g-spot and I moaned. I was tight and sensitive and I couldn't take it, but still Phin wouldn't stop.

This one was a slow buildup. The tension winding so slowly I didn't even notice I was nearing orgasm until I was on the edge. Until the pressure hit me suddenly and I gasped, pressing myself into the feeling.

That was when Phin sped up the invisible cock, slamming it hard and deep and fast until I was a writhing mess.

"Phin, please!" I begged. He reached forward and put pressure on my clit with his paw and that was it. I exploded.

My hands were suddenly free, and I dug them into the blankets at my side as I curved into myself at the overwhelming sensation. I was moaning and panting and writhing, and I wanted the feeling to stop and I never wanted it to stop. White exploded behind my eyes and everything went quiet for a brief moment.

"There you are, little warrior." Phin moved to snuggle beside me. I curved into his warmth and flung my arm and leg over him. He was soft and warm. His arm slid under my neck and rubbed circles onto my back. "That's my good girl. You did so good for me."

Chapter Nine

We laid there for a long while, just enjoying the warming and soothing feeling of his paw on my back. I was dozing off when Phin pulled away from me.

"Shhh, it's okay. I'll be right back." He nuzzled his face into my hair before sliding out from under me and off the bed. I was in a twilight. My body heavy, and languid from the multiple orgasms. My brain sluggish. I was sliding into sleep when Phin returned. He had the baking sheet again, and he gently set it on the bedside table before nudging me awake.

"Here, my little warrior, you need to drink some water. Eat something. Your body will thank you for it tomorrow." I struggled to sit up, straightened my clothes the best I could.

I took the glass of water from between Phin's paws and gratefully drank it. My mouth and throat were dry and the water instantly soothed it. I finished the glass before setting it on the table and investigating the rest of the tray. There was a plate with lunch meat and cheese cubes, a bowl of mixed berries, and a glass of orange juice.

"You're spoiling me." I said, taking the bowl of berries. I didn't stop to consider why the demon might be doing so much for me. Instead, I just enjoyed it. The feeling of being taken care of for a change; was nice.

"You deserve to be spoiled. Finish your berries and I'm going to run you a bath. You've earned it." He brushed a gentle paw over my hair before leaving for the bathroom.

I didn't want to get used to the feeling of being taken care of. I didn't want to have someone doing things for me. What happened if I got used to it and then I was left on my own again?

As the only child of a single parent, I had grown-up young. Oftentimes, I'd had to take care of myself while my mom was working two jobs. I'd learned to get myself around for school, scrounge food for dinner. I'd help around the house because Mom was so exhausted she couldn't do it all.

I was about thirteen when she'd met my step-father and remarried. He was good to her and when they got married. Mom was able to switch to working one job. But she still did the majority of the labor around the house. It worked for them and I was happy for my mom, who was genuinely happy in her marriage.

Still, nothing in my life had prepared me for

someone taking care of my needs. It was weird and made me vaguely uncomfortable. I felt like I was waiting for the other shoe to drop. Except I already knew the other shoe was a one-way trip to Hell.

Still, I let Phin wrangle me into the bathroom to take a bath. I let him insist I drink more water before bed. And when he climbed in beside me, I let myself enjoy his warmth.

Because, just for one day, I wanted to feel like someone actually cared about my needs and that I actually mattered.

It was the first Thanksgiving since my mom remarried, and I didn't have anything to do. When I was married, Tyler insisted we host the meal every year. Though he never helped with preparing it or the house for his whole family.

I had planned on taking the kids to see my mom for the holiday. But the drive didn't feel worth the effort, now that the girls were with their dad. Clover had invited me to celebrate with her and Candy, but I wasn't a hundred percent comfortable with her demon. Which felt a little hypocritical after waking up wrapped around Phin for the second morning in a row.

But I never claimed to be a good person.

There was no point in cooking the full meal for myself. I'd briefly considered ordering in, but I would have had to do that weeks ago and Tyler hadn't given me the warning.

In the end, I ended up spending the morning in bed. I got myself a mug of tea and some buttered toast and went back to bed with my e-reader.

Phin had disappeared somewhere, so it was just me and my book. The quiet was both nice and unsettling. I wasn't used to just being able to exist without having to be on for two little girls at the drop of a hat. Relaxing did not come easily or naturally to me.

By mid-afternoon, I had finished my book and was getting bored with my own company. I thought about calling Clover to see if she still wanted to do something, but she wasn't a fan of last-minute plans. She sometimes struggled with just leaving her home and I hated setting off any of her triggers just because I was incapable of being alone with myself.

I got up and gathered my dishes. That was something I could do. I hadn't paid much attention to the kitchen in the last couple of days and I knew there had to be at least a sink of dishes. I could probably do a load of laundry. There was always laundry in a house with kids.

Except, the kitchen was clean when I got downstairs. There had been the dishes from the tray Phin brought me last night in the sink this morning, but they were gone. The counters had all been wiped down. There was more of the toxic sludge coffee in the coffee pot.

I made a mental note to get a second coffee pot. I couldn't go without coffee, but there was no way I could drink Phin's coffee.

The thought froze me.

What the hell? I was planning to accommodate Phin's terrible coffee habit? I wanted the demon gone. I didn't want to be buying small appliances for him.

Shaking my head, I rinsed my mug and plate and loaded them into the dishwasher. Okay, I could do laundry.

The laundry baskets were empty. The washer was empty. The dryer was running. What the hell?

I kept wandering the house for something to do, but it was all done. Every chore that I could come up with had already been done. Now I knew what the demon had been up to while I was lying in bed.

But where was the damn demon?

The barn, apparently. I had bought an old farmhouse with my divorce settlement. There was a barn the previous owners had maintained just enough to keep it weatherproof but had never done much with it. I used it for yard tool storage and figured I could park my car out there in the winter.

The doors would be a pain in the ass, but it had to be better than scraping windows every morning.

I found Phin in there, tossing a bag of trash into the bin. He wasn't touching the bag or the bin. It took me a moment to process what I was seeing. I knew he had powers; he'd used them in front of and on me before. But nothing so visual.

"What are you doing?" I asked, not sure why I suddenly felt annoyed and angry at him.

"Taking out the trash." He said it with a 'duh' in his tone, which only made me angrier.

"Why? Why did you..." I waved my arm back toward the house.

The lid on the trash can closed and Phin turned to face me fully. Not for the first time, I wished he wasn't stuck in a giant teddy bear body. I couldn't read his expression and there was definitely a look on his face.

"It needed to be done," he said with a shrug. "You should have enough time for a bath before dinner, if you'd like."

"Dinner?" There hadn't been anything cooking inside. And who would be delivering on Thanksgiving outside of fast-food joints?

"Trust me." He sounded exasperated. A small part of me felt bad for being so suspicious and defensive about him doing nice things for me. A large part of me had her back up. He was the one coming in and taking over my life. He didn't belong here. It wasn't natural or normal. What was I supposed to do with him? How would I explain him to my daughters when they got home in two days?

Hi girls, this is Phin. He's a demon and in ten months he's going to take my soul to Hell because I cannot be bothered to find someone to love me.

Yeah, that'd go over well.

"I can see you spiraling. I'm not up to anything nefarious. It's my job to take care of you. I like taking care of things." He came over and rested his paws on my arms, rubbing up and down gently. "Please, just trust me. Have I done anything to make you doubt me?"

"You sent us to a queer speed dating event yesterday."

"Okay, there was that."

"You pinned me to my bed last night."

"Yeah, but you liked that." Phin stepped into my space and somehow, despite me having inches of height on him, he loomed large around me. His voice dropped to a growl. "Tell me you didn't and I'll call you a liar."

I shook my head slowly, unable to honestly deny it. He was right. He'd done nothing to hurt me so far. And as far as we could find, the deal said our demon babysitters couldn't harm us. Besides, a part of me did feel safe with him.

We still had things to talk about and consider. I still wasn't comfortable with him coming in and taking over my house. I didn't like him controlling my life. But I could be gracious. I took a couple of steps back, away from his weirdly looming presence.

"I'm going to clean my room and grab a shower." I started to turn away from him, but stopped. "Thank you for everything."

Chapter Ten

"Why do we do this to ourselves?" I asked Fern as we stood in the mile long line waiting to check out.

"Because we love your girls, and I love you," Fern replied. "Besides, it's tradition."

That was true.

Fern and I had been going Black Friday shopping together for years. Clover hated crowds and her anxiety couldn't handle it. Violet claimed there was nothing she needed enough to deal with the type of people who went out that day. Although it didn't stop her from asking us to pick up things every year.

Fern and I had started shopping together right after college and never stopped. We had a system in place to make sure we got our big-ticket items, often being the first to the stores in the morning. We'd always end the day with a late brunch.

Going to the stores was becoming less necessary with the rise of internet deals but we still, mostly, liked going.

It was highly possible I was insane.

"Tell me about your Thanksgiving." Fern said, moving a few steps forward as the line moved.

I didn't know where to start. I'd come down from my shower to find my meal spread out on the coffee table in the living room. How Phin had managed to get a dinner delivered on Thanksgiving, I couldn't even begin to guess. Given the fact he was a demon, I chose not to think too hard on it.

Alongside the turkey and mashed potatoes was a bottle of my favorite red wine. He had queued up a Christmas romance movie and watched the entire thing with me without complaining. He even debated points of the movie with me, like the complete unbelievability of someone falling head over heels in love over the course of a single weekend.

I drank the wine. I ate the dinner, and the pumpkin pie. When I was done, Phin snuggled me up to his side, letting me use him as a heated pillow. He hadn't once brought up the bargain or how I needed to be dating.

If he wasn't a demon cursed into a crochet bear, it would have been the perfect date night.

As it was, I was confused about Phin. I was starting to like having him around, and I just didn't know how to process that. So, all I could do when Fern asked was to say it was nice and change the subject to her holiday.

By some unspoken agreement, neither of us talked about our devil's bargain or guardian demons. We talked about the upcoming events at the school where she taught kindergarten and where my girls were in second and fourth grade. We talked about our friends, about Clover and Candy.

"Tell me you like your demon," Fern burst out over brunch. "Because I think mine is actually kind of nice, and sweet, and I like having him around. But he's a minion of Hell and there's the whole 'here to steal my soul' thing."

"Yes," was all I could say. "Yes, I like my demon."

'Like' felt like a weak word to explain how I was feeling about my demon.

It was just the only word I had.

Chapter Eleven

P hin was in the bedroom when I got home. I had put away all of my purchases, hiding the Christmas gifts in a horse stall in the barn. When he didn't come to greet me, I went looking for him.

I really didn't like how quickly I had gotten used to him just being there. It was dangerous, in many ways.

"Hey, I was thinking — what in the ever-loving fuck is that?" I stumbled to a stop when I walked in and saw my bed. Spilled across the surface were a number of sex toys and accessories. There was a half-gallon bottle of lube.

Who needed that much lube?

People at orgies, that was who. And I had zero interest in participating in an orgy.

"You'll have to be more specific," Phin said, looking over the bed. I could feel the pleased smugness coming off of him in waves. He thought he was slick and that we would be using any of that.

Nope.

Nope, nope, nope.

Holy shit, that dildo was the size of my forearm. Who needed a dildo the size of their forearm? How did that even work?

Nope. Was not thinking about it.

Oh fuck, I couldn't stop thinking about it.

"This!" I waved my arms at the bed in a flailing gesture. "Where did this come from? Why did this come? Just...why?"

"They came from the internet. I bought them." His voice stopped being amused and grew gravel. "Because you're going to love all the things I can do to you."

"But... I... uh..." It wasn't often I was at a loss for words but I couldn't come up with anything to say to that. Did I even want to encourage him? We weren't like Clover and Candy. He wasn't my demon boyfriend. We'd only known each other for three days.

Holy shit, we'd only known each other for three days.

"Don't worry, warrior. I won't do anything you don't like."

I shook my head. I was not on board with this. I didn't think . . . My eyes went back to the giant dildo. It was pink with silver sparkles. Why? Why did it sparkle?

"Have I ever done anything you didn't like?" He came toward me, running hot paws down my arms. "I just want to make you feel good. You can let me do that, can't you?"

He buried his nose into my neck and I could feel him smelling me. A low grumble moved through his chest and into mine. I could feel that sound everywhere.

"I'm limited in this form. Watching you come is a pleasure. But I want to touch you, I want to make you come with my hands. I want to watch you come on my cock, or as close to it as I can do while I'm stuck like this." He moved his paws up to kind of cup my breasts. I wanted more.

"Fine." I stepped back and pulled my sweater over my head. "But you're not using that pink one on me."

"Whatever you say, little warrior."

I grumbled a bit over the smugness in his voice, but I undid my jeans and slid them down my hips and off. After a moment of hesitation, I slid my underwear off and removed my bra. I felt exposed sitting there naked and unable to read Phin's expression. Goddess, I wish I could read his face.

"You are beautiful." He came to stand in front of me, forcing his way between my legs. He raised a paw to my face, and it was so warm and so sweet, I felt myself melting, just a little bit. It was dangerous and useless, but I couldn't deny it.

"Lay back, lovely." Phin crawled onto the bed as I moved back to lie against the pillows. "Trust me."

It was dumb. It was dangerous. It was insane. But I did trust the damn demon.

He picked up a lemon-yellow cordless wand using both paws and somehow managed to turn it on. He set the toy against my thigh. The soft vibrations startled me even as I expected it.

"Relax."

Easier said than done. I'd never done anything like this. Tyler had seen toys as competition and I'd never had one before. And having it used on me by a giant teddy bear was just ridiculous.

I started giggling. I couldn't help it. The giggles turned into outright laughter and soon I was shaking with it. Oh, my goddess, what the hell was I doing?

My laughter stopped suddenly when Phin moved the wand between my legs. The low vibration had been turned up. My body arched off the bed in surprise. Phin moved, adjusted himself to sit between my legs so I couldn't close them. He held the wand against me, direct vibrations to my clit.

It seemed to take forever, and no time at all before my body was swamped with pleasure. I could feel it in every cell of my body. It pooled in my belly, it tensed in my back, it curled my toes, it fisted my hands in the blankets. I was panting and moaning and begging for it to stop. Begging for more.

I was a mess. And Phin wouldn't let up. Every time I tried to move, he followed me. Keeping the pressure on and the vibrations kept changing, keeping me on edge. I needed to come. I needed a break.

I needed, I needed, I needed...

Every muscle in my body drew tight just as the first wave of pleasure broke over me. White exploded behind my eyelids. My vagina clenched on nothing, and I whined. I was right there, but I couldn't quite reach it when I was so empty.

"Does my girl need more?" Phin asked, pulling the wand away. "I can't fuck you how I want, but you can ride me. You can take what you need from me."

I didn't understand. I struggled to open my eyes and look at him. Somehow, he had gotten a black harness on and attached to it was a light blue dildo. It wasn't as long or as scary as the pink one. It was wider, and I knew the stretch would be intense.

I wanted it.

Phin leaned back against the end of the bed as I clambered to my knees and climbed up his crochet body. The soft chenille yarn felt fantastic against my overstimulated skin.

I straddled his hips and grasped the blue phallus. I was wet. So wet. But still...

The lube was within reach, so I spread some over the fake cock. Tossing the ridiculously over-sized bottle aside I grasped it in one hand and lined it up.

"Oh, my goddess!" I groaned, the size of the dildo almost too much for me. I had to go slowly to allow myself time to stretch around it.

"The way you look right now," Phin groaned. "One day I will see your cunt swallow my dick like that, but this is the next best thing."

His paws went to my hips, pressing me down and against him. I couldn't stop my moan. I had never been so full in my life.

I couldn't help but move against and over him. It didn't take me long to get back to the edge. I was grinding into him when he picked up the wand and slid it back between my legs.

I exploded.

My pussy clamped down on the silicone cock so hard it was almost painful. My entire body was shaking from pleasure. It took effort to get my hands to release the death grip I had on Phin's shoulders. My knees were locked. I fell forward, resting my head on the pillow near Phin's.

"You are so fucking perfect." He said, nuzzling against my neck. He pulled the wand away and turned it off. His arms went around me, holding my shaking body to him. The air was cool against my bare back, but Phin was so warm and his soft body so cozy, his motions soothing. I allowed myself a few moments to bask in sensation and emotion.

Slowly, my body came down and my legs started to cramp up in the bent position they were in. I gently rose up and off of Phin. I winced a little as the dildo pulled free of me. It really had been almost too wide for me.

I helped him remove it from the harness and took it, and the wand, to the bathroom with me. I may not have had any experience with sex toys, but even I knew they needed to be washed after that.

Once I'd taken care of myself and cleaned the toys, I pulled on my robe and headed back into the bedroom. Phin had cleared the rest of the bed off and pulled back the blankets. He was nowhere to be seen.

I crawled into the bed and was just getting comfy when my phone rang. I groaned and got up to get it out of my pants pocket. My daughter's name filled the screen.

"Hey baby, what's up?" I asked, already knowing something was wrong. We'd talked daily since they left, but never in the middle of the day. They'd been too active.

"I want to come home." Thalia cried into the phone. The older of my girls, at eight, Thalia was always the more dramatic of the two.

"You're coming home in two days, sweetheart. What happened?" I climbed back into the bed and tried to keep calm.

"Dad is stupid and I hate him. And I hate Jessica. And I hate Mimi and Papa! I hate everyone and I just want to come home!" She started crying into the phone and my heart ached for her. I made sure that my robe was covering everything and my hair wasn't too crazy before turning the call to video chat.

"Tell me everything."

Chapter Twelve

"I have water, juice, fruit, and yogurt," Phin said, carrying the tray into the bedroom. "I wasn't sure if you'd eaten and what you'd be in the mood for."

I was pulling on my clothes when he came back. After I'd talked to Thalia and Callista I'd called Tyler and told him to get the kids on the plane. There was a direct flight taking off that night and I'd meet them at the other end. I wasn't thrilled about them flying alone at six and eight, but it was better than them staying there any longer with their negligent father.

Tyler had been pissed I'd called and made arrangements without his permission, declaring that it was his weekend. But Thalia's phone uploaded straight to the cloud and I had the video of him screaming at our six -year-old daughter until he was purple in the face. I was not leaving them alone with him any longer than I had to. When I pointed out the courts would love to see the video, as would his bosses at the law firm, he'd hung up on me.

"What's wrong? What's going on?" Phin set the tray on the bedside table and put his paws on my arms.

"I have to go get my girls. I can't believe I let them go with that man."

I shrugged away from him and yanked my shirt over my head. "I know what he's like and still I let him take them."

"He didn't leave you much choice," Phin said. "You tried to tell him it wouldn't be as easy as he thought."

I stopped and stared at him. "How would you even know that?"

"I've been here for a while, Jasmine." He fell back to sit on the bed. "I figured out right away you wouldn't like the girls knowing about me, so I stayed silent until I had a chance to talk to you without them."

He'd been there. He'd been watching me. A part of me was so angry at the invasion of my privacy. But he was right. I would have been more upset if the girls had figured out he was there. Between the two options, he'd picked the best one.

He'd sat there, immobile, for who knows how long, so he wouldn't upset me or startle my kids. That demon, that complete stranger, showed me more thought and consideration before we'd even met than my ex-husband ever had.

I sat on the bed next to him and pulled on my

boots. My heart ached but I knew what I had to do next.

"I need you to leave." I said quietly. "I have to go pick up my girls and bring them home. And I need you not to be here when I get back. They can't know about you and I can't stand knowing you're sitting there completely aware and unable to move."

"You obviously know how to get a hold of my friends. Have one of them come and pick you up if you can't go back wherever you came from. I just...you can't be here when I get back. I'm sorry."

I pushed to my feet and slipped my phone back into my pants pocket. I grabbed my brush to deal with the sweat and sex-tangled mess.

"I can't just go away." Phin grabbed my arm and used it to spin me to face him. "I'm here with you until you find your mate. I can't help you if I'm living with your friend, and I can't go back to where I came from until I'm successful. It would be bad for all of us if I tried."

My throat was tight and my breath was stuck in my chest. I didn't know why this hurt so much. He was a demon. I'd only known him three days.

It didn't matter that in those three days he'd shown me more consideration or care than anyone in my life. That he'd gone out of his way to care for me and my needs. It didn't matter that he'd been responsible for the best sex of my life or that I genuinely enjoyed his company.

None of those things mattered because my

girls would be home in just a couple of hours and he was something I could not explain.

"Phin, you have to go. You can't be here." I threw my brush on the bed and yanked my hair into a messy bun on top of my head. "I can't have you here. You need to be gone by the time the girls and I get back."

I spun and left the room.

Walking away from him hurt, but I had to think of my girls first. They'd been through so much in the last year with the divorce and moving and everything. There was no way I would be able to explain a walking, talking stuffed animal living with us. And I certainly didn't want to have to explain it to anyone else when they inevitably told their classmates or teacher.

It was the right decision. It was the best decision for us.

Goddess, it hurt. It felt like I was losing part of myself.

Stupid fucking emotions.

Chapter Thirteen

The girls weren't on the flight. According to the airline, they'd never checked in on the other side. My emotions warred between panic and anger on the hour-long drive back to my house.

I'd called Tyler more than a dozen times already, cell phone laws be damned, but he never answered. I'd tried calling his parents, but neither of them picked up either. That was less than surprising. They'd never liked me much.

It was full dark by the time I got home, but I could see Tyler's car parked at the head of my driveway by the porch light. All remaining sense of fear turned into a combustible rage at the sight of it.

The car had barely stopped before I had the door open and was lunging out of my car at him. He was moving equally fast, clearly spoiling for a fight.

Good.

I'd give him what he wanted. My body was shaking with pent-up anger and upset. I'd barely managed to keep myself from crying on the drive to the airport, hurting over sending Phin away. I'd waited for almost an hour only to find out my girls weren't even on the plane. The emotional mixture was potent and unstable, and I was ready to brawl.

"Where the fuck have you been?" Tyler asks. "We've been here for thirty minutes."

"I was at the airport. The one I told you to send my daughters to. Imagine my shock when they told me they never even checked in, in Orlando." I marched up to him, ready to strike. "What the actual fuck, Tyler?"

"Jessica was ready to come home. We flew together into Lansing. Which was much safer, don't you think, than having our children fly alone?"

I took a deep breath. I couldn't hit him. He'd take any opportunity to make my life hell, and I couldn't give him one. But my hands were fisted at my sides and I was struggling not to take a swing. Consequences be damned.

"I don't know. Are they safe with you? It sure as fuck didn't look like it in the video the girls sent me."

Tyler grabbed my upper arms and drove me back into the side of the porch. My breath whooshed out of me at the impact. I tensed, waiting for more.

His face was red and there was violence in his eyes.

Instead of pain, Tyler lurched away from me.

No, he was pulled away from me. Tyler wasn't a small man at six feet, but the man pulling him away from me towered over my ex-husband by at least six inches. He was muscular, as evident by his fitted long-sleeve t-shirt. His hair was shaggy and dark.

I watched as he slammed Tyler into the side of his own car, wondering who the hell he was.

"You will not touch her again." The voice was a low growl that settled deep in my chest.

Phin.

This was Phin.

Holy fucking shirtballs.

"You will not touch her. You will not look at her. You will not contact her. If your daughters decide they want to contact you, they will. Until then, you do not exist." He pulled Tyler away from the car and shoved him back against it again. "Do you fucking understand me?"

Phin's arm was across Tyler's throat, pinning him in place.

"He can't speak." I said, my voice higher than usual. I was a maelstrom of emotion.

"He doesn't need to." Phin growled. "Get the girls out of the car, Jasmine."

Oh goddess! I hadn't even thought about the girls in the car. I'd been so angry and emotional and I let it get the better of me. I took a deep breath and walked around to the opposite side of Tyler's car to open the back passenger door.

"Hey babies, how about we go inside now?" I kept my voice soft and calm, though I wasn't feeling anything like it. "Can you get your bags?"

The girls were both crying and threw themselves out of the car at me. I tumbled back onto my butt with a hundred-odd pounds of hysterical children on my lap.

"Shh, shh, shh, it's going to be okay. Let's get your bags and go inside."

I helped gather their suitcases and carry-on bags, and led them in a wide berth around where Phin had Tyler pinned. I waited until they were in the house before turning back to them. "Don't kill him."

With that, I went into the house and locked the door behind me.

Chapter Fourteen

It was well after eleven before I got both girls to sleep. They'd cried and told me all about their trip. Which appeared to have been a mix of fun things with Mimi and Papa, whining from Jessica, and anger from Tyler.

After they'd cried it out and finished the milk and cookies I had pulled out, because every bad day needs comfort food, I'd gotten them into the bath. They were really too old to bathe together anymore, but I'd put them in my oversize tub and let them fill it with lavender bubbles and just relax for a while. The bath and the talking did their job, and they'd finally let me tuck them in with a few chapters of the fantasy novel we were reading.

I was mentally and emotionally drained when I headed back downstairs.

"Are they okay?" The low voice startled me. I whirled toward the kitchen where Phin in his six-and-a-half-foot glory, leaned against the doorframe. He held out a glass of red wine. "I'm sorry if I scared them."

"They'll be okay." I ignored the wine and walked into his chest. I wrapped my arms around his torso and held tight. There were questions I needed answers to very soon but right that minute I just needed a hug.

"It's okay, little warrior." He rubbed my back in a firm circle and I relaxed into his heat. "You're okay."

I took a deep shuddering breath and stepped back to look up at him. "How?"

Phin didn't answer right away. He took my hand and led me into the kitchen where some meat, cheese cubes, and crackers were laid out. After setting my glass down next to one I assumed was for him he backed me into the counter.

"You finally caught up." Phin said, gripping me around the hips and easily lifting me to sit on the island. I took a moment to appreciate the show of strength before going back to my question.

"Caught up to what?"

"That you're perfect for me." A grin tugged up the corner of his mouth. "I've known it since before I said my first words to you. I've just been waiting for you to figure it out, too."

He leaned in and kissed me. It seemed ridiculous that, after all we'd done, this was our first kiss. I pulled back.

"Wait a minute. Clover had to summon the

actual devil to get Candy back. How come you just came back?"

"Candy was coming back either way." He sounded amused. "The drama that summoning caused was the talk of Hell for weeks. Humans, so impatient."

"Well, how were we supposed to know?" I flailed my arms. It wasn't like the deal we'd made with Lucifer had been clear. We hadn't even realized we'd been making a deal when we'd cast the spell all those weeks ago. We'd just been having a laugh.

"I'm still waiting, you know." Phin pressed his palms on the island to either side of me, effectively blocking me in.

"Waiting for what?"

"For you to say it." Phin pressed his lips to my neck, just below my ear. He moved his lips slowly down the column to my shoulder, leaving a trail of fire-hot kisses.

"Say what?" My voice was breathy. The sensation of his mouth on me, along with the heat he emanated everywhere, was a powerful combination.

"I'm here. There's only one thing that can mean." Phin bit lightly into my shoulder. "It means you've accepted that I'm your mate. That you're all mine."

Something occurred to me and I jerked away to glare at him. "You sent us to that queer speed dating event on purpose, didn't you?"

Phin's grin was quick and wicked. He didn't say anything, but I knew. I knew it! That jerk.

"Nope, something must have gotten mixed up because I'm pretty sure I don't even like you." Phin growled and lunged at me. He forced me back onto the island and loomed over me, using his arms to hold him up.

"Little liar." He kissed me then, slow and deep. I wrapped my legs around his hips and kissed him back. His mouth was fire on mine as our tongues danced for dominance.

I used my legs around his hips to grind against him. He was hard and even through our clothes, I knew he was big.

Phin pulled away suddenly and gripped the front of my t-shirt. He yanked and the material split in half.

"Hey!"

"I'll buy you a new one." His head ducked to take my nipple into his mouth as he began undoing my jeans. I couldn't help but moan when he switched breasts. The cool air on my nipple after the intense heat of his mouth was a shock to the system.

He had my jeans undone and was pulling them down as far as he could without stopping. I pushed him away and gripped my pants.

"Off," I demanded. "Take them off."

I shimmied out of my own pants and underwear. There was a moment's thought that we probably shouldn't be doing this in the kitchen, but it was gone the moment Phin had his pants off.

He had the most impressive cock I had ever seen. It was wide and long and I had no clue how it was going to fit inside me, but I was game to try. I was already so wet and ready for him.

When he lined up with my entrance, I pushed back against him. "Condom."

"We don't need it." He rocked forward a little. "Demons can't have children, and we don't carry disease. You're safe."

He pressed deeper, leaning back so he could watch his cock disappear into me. It was slow. So, so slow. I pressed forward against him, but he grabbed my hips to stop me.

"We're going to do this at my pace, love." He gritted his teeth as he pushed forward. "You'll take what I give you."

He reached up and pinched my nipple. I jolted, his grip just this side of painful. But it was a good pain. Something I hadn't even known I would like until that moment.

"More." I demanded. Phin silenced me with a kiss. He kissed deep as he finished sliding all of the way into me before slowly sliding out again all the way to the tip.

He kept up that slow slide and that deep kiss for what felt like forever. My entire body was flashing hot. I was shaking with sensation and the need to come. I wanted more of him. Harder. Faster. Anything to send me rocketing over the edge into orgasm.

"Listen to you beg." Phin said, pulling away. He leaned back so he could watch us again. "Mm, look at you taking my cock so well."

His thumb was a ghost of sensation over my clit, but it was enough to make me moan and beg for more. Which only made Phin laugh.

I was ready to lose my mind when suddenly he pressed his thumb down on my swollen bud. At the same time, he slammed his cock into me. I screamed and immediately covered my mouth with my hand. I didn't want to wake the girls. I certainly didn't want them to see me like this. But it felt so, so good.

Phin's movements were fast and hard as he fucked into me. It was too much. It was not enough. It was perfect. I never wanted it to end, but it didn't take long before the excess of sensation dragged an orgasm out of me. But Phin kept going. He kept his thumb in firm circles around my clit as he kept thrusting into me.

He kept going until my legs were shaking and I was unable to hold myself up any longer. I was laying back on the kitchen island with my legs hanging loose over the side while a demon fucked me like there was no tomorrow. It was too much. It wasn't enough. It was perfect.

Epilogue

"You can't stay here, you know," I said a while later. Phin and I were curled up on the couch drinking the wine he had poured earlier. "How would I even begin to explain you to the girls? Also, they're a little scared of you after seeing you take out Tyler like that."

"I'm not going anywhere." Phin pressed a kiss to my head and dragged me closer to him.

"Phin–" I began, but he cut me off.

"There's a loft apartment in the barn. It needs some work, but it's mostly livable. I'll stay out there until you're ready to tell the girls about us."

"That place is a mess." I argued.

"It'll be fine."

"You'll freeze!"

"Demon." He pointed to his chest. "I generate enough heat to warm the whole apartment if I need to. But it seems like there is heat installed up there."

I rested my head on his shoulder. He was so,

so warm. Which was a good thing since I was sitting there in nothing but his long-sleeve shirt since he'd ripped mine.

"What do I tell the girls?" I wondered, watching the first few flakes of snow fall outside the window. "Hey, here's this total stranger who's going to be living in our barn and sharing the bathroom with us?"

"Technically, there's a bathroom in the loft."

"Don't be cute." I elbowed him in the side gently. "I'm serious. How do I explain you?"

We were both silent. I don't know if Phin was really thinking about the question or not, but I couldn't let it go. This was my girls we were talking about. They were smart and didn't take bullshit. They'd know something was up.

"Tell them I'm a friend and I'm staying for a while to do some work. Fixing up the loft will give me something to do. I can help around the house." He grabbed my chin and tilted my head to look at him. "I like taking care of you."

His eyes were so dark they were almost pure black. I wondered what his demon form looked like. Clover said Candy looked even better as a demon than she did in her human form and Candy was a smoke show. I wondered if I'd ever get to see it.

"Okay."

Okay to staying. Okay to taking care of me. Okay to living in the loft. Okay to anything and everything.

Bonus Prequel

I had not signed on for this.

Well, technically, I hadn't signed on for anything. It wasn't like Hell gave demons much of a choice.

No, it was all 'hey, welcome to Hell, do you want to spend an eternity being tortured or do you want to go corrupt some others and see what happens?' And then we've got about thirty seconds to decide our future. But honestly, what choice is there?

Not that every soul that ends up in Hell is given a choice. Most weren't. The majority of souls were sent to their eternal torment or left to float in the River Styx. But, for some of us, we were given an out.

I won't lie. I'd enjoyed being a demon. It had been a lot of fun, fucking my way through the centuries. I'd loved the challenge of finding just the right soul to lure to lust. Sure, I'd been getting bored recently, but it'd been a few hundred years of fucking and even lust grew old.

Honestly, I'd been glad when my demon lord had recalled me to Hell for a special assignment. Confused, but glad. In all the time I'd been a demon, I'd been called in front of Asmodeus once, when I'd first been changed. I was low-level at best. High enough in the hierarchy, I didn't have to worry about being mistaken for one of the palace slaves, but low enough that no one knew who I was. I did my job, culled my souls, and spent the rest of the time lying low in my rooms.

My confusion only grew when I was told I wasn't to cull the woman I was being sent to, but to protect her. To help her find love. It was the most bizarre order I'd ever been given. I was a lust demon. What the fuck did I know about love?

Still, when the demon lord demands you're going to help a woman find love, you're going to help a human woman find love. Well, unless you wanted to end up in the depths of Hell being tortured for the next century or two until he remembered you existed.

No, thank you.

But it would have been really fucking nice to know I would not be heading to earth in my corporeal body. No, I'd be taking the form of a giant fucking teddy bear.

Getting there to learn that fact had been a lot of fun. I was sure Asmodeus was laughing his ass off down there. Especially when I learned the woman had kids. I may have been a demon, but I wasn't going to freak the fuck out of a couple of little kids by getting up and walking around. That was some horror movie level childhood trauma shit.

Unfortunately, that meant a lot of sitting. And waiting. And watching.

The watching was my favorite part. I had been placed in a home office that gave me a lot of time to watch the human I was meant to protect. An activity that quickly became my favorite pastime.

She was a fascinating mix of soft and hard. She could take someone down in a work meeting with a glare and a single sentence. She shut down angry customers without raising her voice. She had a spine of steel. But she would melt the second her girls came into the room. No matter how upset or tired or frustrated she was, she always had time for them and did her best to give them all of the attention they wanted.

I couldn't help but wonder if my life, and afterlife, would have turned out differently if I'd had someone show any of the love and kindness she gave her girls. I couldn't help but think about the coldness of my childhood, the violence and general chaos of it.

After weeks of watching her, I craved her softness. I craved the affectionate and gentle touches. I craved the sharp edges and the soft heart. I simply craved her.

And my job was to help her fall in love with someone else.

***

Jasmine was gloriously pissed off. I laid back in the chair she'd placed me, and watched as she paced her small office and yelled into the phone. Whoever was on the other end, her ex, from the sound of it, wasn't paying attention to her and only seemed to be making her more angry.

I'd seen her a lot of ways in the time I'd spent in that chair, but this was a side to her I hadn't seen before. Her dark eyes flashed with fire and her skin was flushed with the argument. I couldn't stop my mind from wandering to what she might look like flushed for other reasons. Would the color on her cheeks spread down her chest? Would her dark eyes go bright when she was flushed with arousal? I'd spent too much time wondering what she would look like in the throws of passion.

"Doesn't seem like I have a fucking choice, does it? See you Wednesday." I watched Jasmine hang up and toss the phone on the desk before sinking into the desk chair. She leaned forward, elbows on her knees, and drove her fingers into her hair. She fisted the strands, and I wanted to go soothe her.

I could. No kids were around. I could let her know I was there and make her feel better. I shifted, on the verge of getting up, but Jasmine sat up and dropped her hands and I froze. Not because I didn't want to get up, but because she looked so stressed and upset. And so very tired.

Not the kind of tired fixed by a good night of

sleep. The kind of bone-deep wariness that sunk into bones and dug into the soul. No, it wasn't the time.

With no small amount of pride, I watched as she pulled herself together and plastered a smile on her face when the door opened and the kids came rushing in, home from school and ready to talk about their adventures of the day. And just like that, she was back in mom mode and my window of opportunity was over.

Truth be told, there had been plenty of chances over the weeks that I could have altered her to my presence. The late nights she spent pouring over spreadsheets after the girls went to bed, the early mornings she came in to get just a little more work done before she woke up the girls.

I could have told her a thousand times over, but I didn't want to add to her burden. I didn't want to see her shoulders slump under the weight of my presence. So I sat, and I watched, and I waited.

Eventually, I would have to alert her to my presence. And then everything would change. I had no doubt about it.

***

My moment had come. I listened as Jasmine got her girls out the front door. My entire body was tense as I listened to the clipped and annoyed tones of her ex-husband's voice as it carried up the stairs. I wanted nothing more than to go down there and put the asshole in his place. But that would only create more issues for Jasmine, and that was the last thing I wanted to do.

As the voices settled and moved outside, I pushed up from the chair and slowly moved my way to the stairs. I was fairly certain I could manage them, but the body I was stuck in was awkward and unbalanced. Only my demon powers made the legs strong enough to hold me up.

I remained silent as I stood at the top of the stairs and waited until I could hear the roar of the car in the driveway before starting my slow descent. My heart ached when Jasmine sagged against the open door frame and watched the car head down the drive.

I had planned a soft opening, but I didn't think that would work under those circumstances. So I said the first thing that came to my mind. Something that would straighten her spine and hopefully put some of the fire back into her.

"Good grief, I thought they would never leave." Jasmine jumped and spun around. She was startled, but she was also pissed. I could see the rage growing inside of her, and I loved it.

"I take it you're my demon."

Fuck yes, I was. I would be her anything if she'd let me. But I knew she wasn't claiming me. She'd made her opinion on the spell that brought me here and the demons they'd summoned very clear in her phone calls with her friends. I was under no illusion.

But that didn't stop me from putting it all out

there. I raised my eyebrows with a sardonic grin that I was sure didn't translate in my teddy bear form and put my wildest fantasy into the universe.

"I guess that makes you my human."

Acknowledgments

First and foremost, thank you to everyone who picked up this weird little book and made it to this point. You have no clue how much each and every one of you means to me.

To everyone who read Corny and reviews it, posted about it, cheered me on while writing Snuggle: I love you. You have no idea what that kind of support means to a new author.

To J, A, E, & C: Thank you for letting me talk endlessly about my weird little books and melt-down and squee and be generally annoying about my demon stuffes.

To J: Thanks for the endless candy corn memes and awkward hot dog GIFs. You're simply the best.

B: Thank you for making my writing better. For letting me talk through every plot hole and writer's block at the weirdest hours. For telling me to STFU and write when I'd rather whine about how hard writing is.

Mom: I'm sorry. I'm so, so sorry. But really, you raised me and have no one to blame but yourself.

About the Author

Sabrina Cross (she/her) is a neurospicy 80's baby from the middle of nowhere Michigan, where she still lives with her cat. She came into her monster romance era early when she fell in love with Beast from the 1997's X-Men animated series. After discovering sentient object romance in early 2023, Sabrina decided to embrace what she calls her 'Hold My Beer' style of writing and gave into the lifelong dream of being an author. When not writing weird monster/sentient object smut, Sabrina can be found hanging out on social media (@authorsabrinacross), reading, or hoarding office supplies.

Also by Sabrina Cross

Yarn & Monsters Series

A True Love Spell Gone Wrong...

When four friends perform a true love spell, things go terribly wrong. Now they're locked into a deal with the devil and have only a year to find love and happiness or their souls are destined to face the flames. Armed with a demon guardian; Clover, Jasmine, Fern, and Violet are determined to beat the devil and save themselves. Except, this curse might be the best thing that's ever happened to them.

Corny: A F/F Candy Corn Romance

A True Love Spell Gone Wrong...

A Demon Fairy Godmother?

Her very soul on the line. Can Clover still find true love or is she destined to face the flames alone?

Snuggle: A M/F Demon Teddy Bear Romance

A True Love Spell Gone Wrong...

Jasmine is too busy to go to Hell and she's definitely too busy for demon antics. But when her demon "Fairy Godmother" shows up, everything is on the line. Does she have what it takes to get out of the Devil's bargain or is she doomed to face the flames?

Tangled: A M/F Friends-To-Lovers Sentient Object Romance

A True Love Spell Gone Wrong…

Fern is going to Hell. Not metaphorical Hell but actual, physical Hell. But there's one thing she needs to do before she goes. An item she desperately needs to scratch off the bucket list. And she's hoping the demon sent to guard her will be willing to help her out.

Knotted: A M/F Demon Werewolf Romance

A True Love Spell Gone Wrong…

Violet was no witch but that didn't stop her from trying to use magic to find love. When the spell backfired and left her and her friends bound in a deal with the devil, Violet vowed to find a solution. Now, with less than two months until the deal comes due and zero leads, she's facing the fire. The fire comes early in the form of a great black beast in her bed. Does Violet find the love she's been looking for or does Hell claim her soul?

Light Me Up

He was the first man to ever turn me on. When he flipped my switch and lit me up that first time, I knew he was it for me. There would never be another.

Pounded by the Pommel Horse

Elena loves being on top. When the elite gymnast is challenged to defeat her gym rival on the pommel horse, she's up for the task. But is she up for the ride when the pommel horse shapeshifts into a man? A very, very naked Man?

Christmas with the Monster

He's Got a Package for Her… Devynn expected her first holiday without her kids to be difficult. But nothing could have prepared her for what she found under the tree just after midnight.With the help of his magic sack, the furry, green giant promises Devynn all kinds of pleasure. But would one night with the Christmas monster ever be enough?

Sentient Pen15 from Outer Space

Liam had spent a lot of his childhood obsessed with the legends of the local mines. The abandoned tunnels underground had driven dozens of workers insane and young Liam was desperate to get to the bottom of it. But he found more than he bargained for down there.

Infected by parasitic space mold, Liam has held himself away from relationships for years. When things spark between him and the girl next door, he has no choice but to reveal the truth: his manly appendage is also the bane of his existence.

www.ingramcontent.com/pod-product-compliance
Lightning Source LLC
Chambersburg PA
CBHW020734310726

48969CB00003B/827